P9-CAJ-441

Lacey
the Little
Mermaid Fairy

A gift from the fairies to Lois Burrows

Special thanks to Mandy Archer

Text copyright © 2016 by Rainbow Magic Limited

All rights reserved. Published by Scholastic Inc., 557 Broadway, New York, NY 10012, *Publishers since 1920*. SCHOLASTIC and associated logos are trademarks and/or registered trademarks of Scholastic Inc. Published by arrangement with Rainbow Magic Limited. Series created by Rainbow Magic Limited. RAINBOW MAGIC is a trademark of Rainbow Magic Limited. Reg. U.S. Patent & Trademark Office and other countries. HIT and the HIT logo are trademarks of HIT Entertainment Limited.

The publisher does not have any control over and does not assume any responsibility for author or third-party websites or their content.

No part of this publication may be reproduced, stored in a retrieval system, or transmitted in any form or by any means, electronic, mechanical, photocopying, recording, or otherwise, without written permission of the publisher. For information regarding permission, write to Scholastic Inc., 557 Broadway, New York, NY 10012.

This book is a work of fiction. Names, characters, places, and incidents are either the product of the author's imagination or are used fictitiously, and any resemblance to actual persons, living or dead, business establishments, events, or locales is entirely coincidental.

ISBN 978-0-545-88742-7

10 9 8 7 6 5 4 3 2 1   16 17 18 19 20

Printed in the U.S.A.   40

First edition, January 2016

Lacey
the Little
Mermaid Fairy

by Daisy Meadows

SCHOLASTIC INC.

The Fairyland Palace

Fairy Tale Lane

Rachel's Hou

Tippington Town

Jack Frost's
Ice Castle

Forest

Tiptop Castle

The Fairy Tale Fairies are in for a shock!
Cinderella won't run at the strike of the clock.
No one can stop me—I've plotted and planned,
And I'll be the fairest one in all of the land.

It will take someone handsome and witty and clever
To stop storybook endings forever and ever.
But to see fairies suffer great trouble and strife,
Will make me live happily all of my life!

Contents

Fairy Tale Castle   1

Mermaid in the Moat   15

Search and Rescue   27

Tickle Time   37

Fairy Tale Emergency   47

A Fairy Tale Ending   57

Fairy Tale Castle

"I'm sure it's this way," said Rachel Walker, pointing to a twisty stone staircase. She lifted a rolled-up banner onto her shoulder and began to tiptoe down the steps.

Kirsty Tate followed behind her best friend. In her arms she was carrying a large cardboard box.

"This must be the east tower," she decided, stopping to peek out of an arched window. Rachel paused to look, too. From where they were standing the girls had a perfect view of Tiptop Castle's courtyard.

Kirsty beamed—it was like a scene from a fairy tale! A fountain carved in the shape of a shell bubbled merrily

in the middle and sweet-smelling pink
roses curled up the columns around the
sides. She wouldn't have been surprised
to glimpse a royal princess wandering
along the walkways or a knight ride in
on a glossy white horse.

"What a magical place," declared
Rachel. "We're so lucky to be
staying here!"

"I wouldn't have missed it for anything," agreed Kirsty, following her friend through an oak archway at the bottom of the stairs.

Rachel and Kirsty had been sharing an amazing spring vacation at Tiptop Castle. Being together was always a dream come true, but this week had been extra-special so far. The friends were taking part in the castle's annual Fairy Tale Festival. They'd spent their days dressing up in beautiful costumes, acting out stories, and drawing pictures of all their favorite characters.

Every night when the fun and games were over, the girls got to sleep in a real castle bedroom! It was a world away from their homes in Tippington and Wetherbury—a place full of tapestries, glittering chandeliers, and four-poster beds with velvet hangings.

The girls stepped out into the castle courtyard.

"The drawbridge is just over there," said Rachel.

Kirsty opened her cardboard box and lifted out the decorations inside: a long string of red and gold flags. Some had stripes and others had polka dots.

"These would look really pretty pinned around the gatehouse," she suggested.

"Good idea," replied Rachel, unfurling a banner. She felt her heart skip when she read WELCOME TO THE FAIRY TALE BALL twinkling in the afternoon light.

Kirsty and Rachel shared an excited smile. Tiptop Castle was celebrating the end of the Fairy Tale Festival with a wonderful party for all of the children who had taken part in the event. Their parents had even been invited to join in, too.

"All the grown-up guests will be here by six," said Rachel, tying the banner to the front gate so that everyone would see it.

Her eyes shone. This had been such an exciting spring vacation! On their very first morning at Tiptop Castle, they had been visited by Hannah the Happily Ever After Fairy. The fairies were Kirsty and Rachel's very special secret. No one else knew about the magical adventures they had shared with Hannah and her friends.

Before they could say "once upon a time . . ." Hannah had shrunk the girls to fairy size and whisked them back to Fairyland. They found themselves fluttering through the air to greet seven beautiful fairies. Each of the Fairy Tale

Fairies took care of a fairy tale and the characters in it. Meeting them had been an honor, especially when they'd presented Kirsty and Rachel with a special book filled with their favorite stories.

Rachel shuddered as she remembered what had happened next. When she'd opened up *The Fairies' Book*  of Fairy Tales, all of the pages had been blank! The Fairy Tale Fairies had realized that their magic objects were missing, plunging their stories into

terrible trouble. The magic objects
were the invisible glue that kept the
characters inside their tales. Without
them, Cinderella and all the others
would slip out and disappear.

It didn't take long to figure out what
had happened to the magic objects. With
an icy blast Jack Frost had appeared. He
bragged that his goblins had swiped the
Fairy Tale Fairies' objects so he could
rewrite all of their stories in the way that
he chose. Noble princes, fair princesses,
and kindly fairies were gone for good.
Instead he cast himself and the goblins as
the stars!

Before Kirsty and Rachel could do
anything to stop him, Jack Frost vanished
to the human world. The Fairy Tale
Fairies were sad. Jack Frost had not

only stolen their magic objects, he'd made off with all of their fairy tale characters, too!

Ever since they'd got back to Tiptop Castle, Kirsty and Rachel had been trying hard to rescue the treasured possessions. They'd managed to return six of the magic objects so far. They'd also helped characters find their way back into the pages of *Sleeping Beauty*, *Snow White*, *Cinderella*, *The Frog Princess*, *Beauty and the Beast*, and *The Princess and the Pea*.

"It really has been an adventure from start to finish," Rachel said.

"It's not over yet," Kirsty reminded her.

Rachel sighed. Poor Lacey the Little Mermaid Fairy was still searching for her magic object! If they didn't find it soon, the festival would be over and the story of *The Little Mermaid* would be ruined forever.

"Come on," said Kirsty, slipping her arm through Rachel's and leading her back inside. "The

decorating's done now. Let's go and get ready for the ball."

The girls made their way across the courtyard, chatting about what to wear. They skipped past the gurgling fountain,

watching the sunbeams dance and glow
in the water.

Rachel's heart began to flutter.

"Kirsty," she whispered. "Look!"

Kirsty had seen it, too. The sunbeams
weren't sunbeams at all! Instead, a
thousand tiny golden bubbles shimmered
in the spray. The girls tiptoed up to the
fountain, and then sat on the stone ledge

that ran around the edge. A little fairy
was splashing in the water! She looked
up and smiled sweetly.

"Hello again!" she exclaimed. "Are
you ready for an adventure?"

Mermaid in the Moat

Kirsty and Rachel recognized Lacey the Little Mermaid Fairy right away—she was just as sparkly as they remembered! Lacey's delicate wings glistened in the sunshine and her mermaid tail sparkled with pale purple scales. Her dark hair was held in place with a fine golden headband. Along the bottom of her shirt a row of tiny jewels glinted in the light.

"We're always ready to help a fairy," whispered Rachel, kneeling over the side of the fountain to make sure that no one else would see Lacey.

"Always," echoed Kirsty. "What can we do?"

Lacey's pretty smile faded. "It's my fairy tale." She sighed. "I can't go on for a minute longer without putting things right!"

"Is there still no sign of your magic object?" wondered Rachel.

Lacey shook her head sadly.

"What does it look like?" asked Kirsty.

"It's an oyster shell with a pearl inside," replied Lacey. "It's very precious.

16

The characters from *The Little Mermaid* have been gone for days now. The shell could be anywhere!"

"We'll find it somehow," promised Rachel.

"There must be somewhere new that we can search," said Kirsty. "Let's think . . ."

"Hey! Over here!"

Lacey and the girls looked up. Someone was shouting from the other side of the courtyard. Another voice bellowed a reply:

"Look at that!"

"It's splashing all over the place!" yelled a third voice.

"Don't just stare at it—let's get it!" boomed another.

Lacey flipped out of the water. "That noise," she cried breathlessly. "It's coming from the moat."

"We need to get there fast!" urged Rachel.

Kirsty began to run, but Lacey shook her head.

"You'll be faster as fairies," she said, pointing her wand into the fountain. As soon as the wand touched the water, a wave of miniature golden shells showered in all directions. Lacey beckoned for the girls to put their hands underneath it. Kirsty and Rachel gazed in wonder as the shells tickled and popped on their fingers before disappearing into the spray. Soon the girls were covered in a sparkling mist of gold.

"We're getting smaller!" exclaimed Kirsty.

When the mist cleared, Rachel reached up to touch her shoulders. A gauzy pair of fairy wings had appeared. The friends joined hands, then fluttered into the air.

"Hey, you!" shouted the voices again. "Come here!"

Kirsty, Rachel, and Lacey hurried across the courtyard, following the noisy shouts. They flew out past the gatehouse, across the drawbridge, and over the moat.

"Oh my!" cried Lacey, nearly tumbling out of the sky. "Goblins!"

Kirsty and Rachel looked down. Floating on the moat, in among the lily pads, was an inflatable raft. Four green goblins were sitting on it, fighting over a giant fishing net.

"She's too heavy!" moaned one goblin, tugging the net with all his might.

"Let me have a try," barked another, shoving his friend out of the way. The goblin heaved and hauled the net until— *plop!*—it landed on the raft. The rest of the gang hooted in delight. A mermaid suddenly popped her head out of the net, then sat up in the middle of the raft.

Lacey gasped. "It's the Little Mermaid from my fairy tale!"

"It figures that the goblins are up to no good." Rachel frowned.

"Why did you do that?" asked the Little Mermaid, pointing at the biggest goblin. "It's not very nice—I don't like being fished out of the water."

The rude goblin stuck out his tongue at her. "We don't care what *you* like," he announced. "We only care about what Jack Frost likes. And he's got a job for you."

The Little Mermaid looked puzzled.

"If he's going to be the star of your fairy tale, he'll need some mermaid lessons," added another goblin, "and who better to teach Jack Frost than the Little Mermaid herself?"

With that, the goblins broke into whoops of laughter.

They sat clutching their sides, laughing at their own cleverness. The Little Mermaid tried to talk to them, but no one would listen to a word she said.

Kirsty flew ahead of Rachel and Lacey.

"We must get down to the raft," she urged, leading the way down to the water's edge.

"We'll have to be careful," warned Lacey.

The brave fairies made their way across the moat, fluttering from lily pad to lily pad. When they got close, they flew up beside the Little Mermaid.

"*Shh,*" whispered Rachel, waving hello. "We're here to set you free."

The Little Mermaid looked at them with relief. "Thank you." She smiled. "Now, if I can just get out of this net . . ."

Kirsty tugged at the cords, but they wouldn't budge. They were wound tight around the mermaid's tail.

"It won't come off," Lacey said, pulling from her end.

Rachel frowned. The Little Mermaid was really caught.

Just then, a huge paddle plunged into the water. Another one dropped down on the other side. The Little Mermaid leaned over the side of the raft, her eyes filled with worry.

"The goblins are rowing away," she whispered urgently. "What am I going to do?"

Lacey watched nervously as the raft lurched downstream.

"We'll find a way to save you somehow," she called.

Search and Rescue

Kirsty, Rachel, and Lacey flew after the Little Mermaid. The silly goblins were so busy paddling, they didn't notice a thing.

"Hurry up!" bellowed the biggest one, nudging his friend in the stomach. "We can't keep Jack Frost waiting!"

"He's going to have to," grumbled the other one. "How am I supposed to row any faster with a big lump like you weighing us down?"

While the goblins squabbled, the Little Mermaid wriggled inside the fishing net. Her face fell when the raft veered out of the moat and into a narrow sidestream.

"They're heading for Tiptop Pond," murmured Rachel, pointing to a pool of water hidden among the trees.

As the Little Mermaid and the goblins rounded the final bend, an old wooden boathouse loomed into view. Kirsty and her friends fluttered into the branches of a willow tree to see what would happen next.

Bang! Clatter!

The boathouse doors were suddenly flung open. The fairies watched in amazement as Jack Frost strutted into view. He was decked out in a mermaid

outfit and swimming cap!
He had water wings on
his arms and a rubber
ring around his middle
that kept slipping down.
Big toes poked out of
the bottom of the
costume where
the mermaid's tail
should have been.
He clutched a trident

in one hand, dripping with jewels and
gold chains. Before Jack spoke to the
goblins, he couldn't resist peeking into
the water to look at his reflection one
more time.

"Splendid," he said, turning around
to admire the sequins that glittered all
over the outfit in icy shades of blue. He

swaggered up and down the bank of the pond, waiting for the goblins to notice him. When they didn't, his face broke into an angry scowl. "Get over here now!" he bellowed.

The goblins paddled so hard that the raft nearly tipped over.

"We got her," squawked the biggest one. "The Little Mermaid."

Jack Frost banged his trident on the ground. The net instantly fell away from the Little Mermaid's tail. She flipped herself into the water, but there was no escape. The goblins made sure that they were blocking the stream that led back to the moat.

"You can leave when you've taught me what I need to know," declared Jack Frost. "I want to act like a mermaid!"

The Little Mermaid glanced up at Lacey, Kirsty, and Rachel. She had no choice. With a big sigh, she began the first lesson.

"We'll start with swimming and tail swishing," she decided. "You do know how to swim, don't you?"

"Humph!" muttered Jack Frost. He made an angry face, then gingerly stepped into the water, still clutching the trident in his fist.

Kirsty waited until Jack Frost was in up to his waist. He tried to do swimming strokes with his arms, but his feet stayed rooted to the ground.

"Let's look inside the boathouse for  your shell," she suggested. "Jack Frost could be here for hours!" One by one, the fairies silently glided toward the shallow edge of the pond. Only the Little Mermaid noticed them go by, doing her best to make sure that Jack Frost faced the other way.

It didn't take long to search the boathouse. The magic scallop shell was nowhere to be seen. The fairies flew back outside, landing gently in a patch of reeds.

"What do we do now?" wondered Rachel, looking across the pond. All the friends could see from their hiding place was the tip of Jack Frost's trident wobbling as he moved.

"He'd swim much better if he put it down," said Kirsty absent-mindedly.

Lacey suddenly gasped in surprise. "Look!" she cried, pushing the reeds to one side. There, in among the priceless gems hanging from the trident, was her magic shell with the pearl inside!

"No wonder he wants to keep the trident close," marveled Rachel.

Lacey nodded happily, then whispered a fairy spell:

A scallop shell, a creamy pearl,
Bubbles gather, bubbles swirl!

Three foamy gold bubbles suddenly
rose out of the pond and floated
dreamily through the air. Kirsty and
Rachel beamed with delight
as the bubbles got closer
and closer to their heads.

"When they touch
you," said
Lacey, "dive
into the
pond.
The
bubbles
will
help you
breathe
underwater."

Kirsty and Rachel did as they were told. Suddenly they felt the bubbles settle on their heads. Instead of popping, they sat on their shoulders like pearly diving helmets.

Rachel dove in after Lacey. She looked back through the emerald-green pond, but Kirsty was nowhere to be seen.

Suddenly a voice rang out through the water.

"Help me, someone!" cried her best friend. "I'm stuck!"

Tickle Time

Rachel and Lacey swam back as fast as they could, a little trail of golden bubbles streaming behind them.

"Over here!" cried Kirsty.

Rachel peered through the dappled water. There was nothing to be seen to the left or right, and only a thick clump of weeds below. She looked again. There was poor Kirsty, stuck right in the middle of it! Somehow the weeds had wrapped around her arms and legs, holding her fast. Lacey reached into the weeds to grab her hand, but they began to tangle up around her, too.

"Don't come any closer," urged Kirsty. "You must get to the trident."

"We're not leaving you," declared Lacey, looking around for help.

"Let's ask those fish!" suggested Rachel.

A school of silvery fish with see-through tails glided in and out of the weeds, nibbling at the stems. As soon as Rachel got close, they darted off in a hundred different directions.

"Please don't be scared," said Lacey. "We won't hurt you—we're fairies."

Slowly and nervously, the fish moved back into the light. The moment they saw Lacey's friendly face and fairy wings they surged forward, swishing their tails excitedly.

Lacey said hello and pointed down to Kirsty. "This weeds are so sticky," she explained. "She's tied up in knots."

"We can help," said a tiny fish with glimmering scales. "We're small, but we're very good at nibbling!"

With that, he darted down into the shadows and started munching on a thick stem. The others all joined in, too.

"That's better!" exclaimed Kirsty, as the stem around her arm broke free. She smiled happily as the fish nibbled the weeds on the other side, too.

"I'll dive down to the lower stems," cried another fish.

"I hope you're not ticklish," piped up a fish with bright eyes.

Kirsty started to giggle. The fish were nibbling the clump of weeds wrapped around her feet.

"Oh my!" she chuckled. "I think I am!"

Working together, the school of fish nibbled Kirsty free in no time.

"Good work!" Lacey laughed.

Rachel's eyes began to twinkle. The fishes' speedy rescue plan had just given her a magical idea . . .

A few moments later, the fairies and their new friends were swimming through Tiptop Pond.

"This way!" called Rachel, pointing to a sandy spot not far from the middle.

The fish darted through the water. The silvery school seemed to move as one big fish instead of lots of tiny ones. They gathered in clusters around two twinkly blue posts—Jack Frost's legs!

Lacey gave the signal with her wand. "One, two, three . . . nibble!"

The fish flitted down to the pond floor, then started tickling and nudging at Jack Frost's pointy toes.

"Aargggh!"
There was
a dreadful
commotion
above the
surface.
Jack Frost
hopped from
foot to foot, slapping
the water with his fists. The goblins
watched, confused as he erupted into
shrieks of laughter.

Underneath the water Kirsty, Rachel,
and Lacey held hands, desperately
hoping that Jack Frost's attack of the
tickles might cause him to drop his
precious trident.

"It's no good." Rachel frowned. "He's
not letting go!"

"We can't give up!" called Kirsty,
swimming down to add some extra
tickles of her own. Lacey joined in, but
Jack Frost still clung to the trident.

Rachel was just about to dive in, too,
when Jack Frost glanced down. He
spotted the fairies and his face filled
with rage.

"What are you doing here?" he
thundered. "I'm trying to have a
mermaid lesson!"

Lacey
summoned
up all her
courage and
popped
her head
out of the
water.

"I'm here for my magic shell," she retorted. "Please give it to me!"

Jack Frost threw his head back and howled with glee.

"This little thing?" he smirked, lifting the trident out of the pond so no one else could reach it. "Well, I want it, so tough luck! You'll never get it back, not now and not ever!"

Fairy Tale Emergency

Lacey's wings drooped and her cheeks turned pale.

"What am I going to do?" she wailed. "My fairy tale will never be the same again!"

The warm golden glow that usually shone around Lacey had faded away to almost nothing. Kirsty and Rachel paddled through the gloom to get to her and gave her a big hug.

"Don't be sad. We never give up on a friend," promised Rachel.

"That's right," agreed Kirsty. She called out in a cheerful voice, "Keep tickling, fish!"

Jack Frost held the trident up as high as he could, but it was getting hard to keep his balance. Splashes rippled through the pond as he wobbled backward and forward. He hooted with giggles, slapping his spare hand through the water to shoo away the fish.

Rachel spotted a broken-off piece of reed floating down to the pond bed. She reached out and grabbed it.

"We've tried the feet," she decided, "so let's move on to the knees!"

Rachel swam up behind Jack Frost, then gently touched the back of one knee with the reed. His legs buckled and kicked—she'd found his ticklish spot!

"Get off!" roared Jack Frost, wildly waving his arms.

Splash!

The trident fell out of his hands, plunging the gems, chains, and magic shell into the water.

"Goblins!" Jack Frost yelled, turning to the raft. "Get over here now!"

"We're coming!" yelled the biggest one. "Get a move on, crew—row in a starboard direction!"

The goblin sitting beside him in the raft scratched his head. "That's forward, right?" he wondered, turning to his friend behind him.

His friend nodded, and then changed his mind. The goblins began to paddle furiously—in different directions! The

raft moved nowhere at all. While Jack Frost's goblins flapped and splashed in the water, someone else swooped in and plucked the trident out of the pond.

"I think this belongs to you," beamed the Little Mermaid, offering it to Lacey.

Lacey's face burst into a dazzling, delighted smile. Quick as a flash she swam up and lifted the special shell off the trident's fork. The instant the fairy touched it, the magic object shrank back down to a tiny size. Lacey pried open the shell and peeked inside— the pearl was still there!

"Well done," she gushed, reaching out to her friends. "We did it after all!"

"Thank you, Kirsty and Rachel," piped up the Little Mermaid. With a farewell wave she was gone, shimmering back into the pages of her story.

Now that her fairy tale characters were back where they belonged, Lacey could sparkle again! She flipped and danced in the water, golden fairy dust glittering all around her.

"I'm so pleased that you were here to save the day," she said gratefully, taking Kirsty's and Rachel's hands.

"We are, too!" agreed the best friends.

Just then, a booming voice thundered across the pond. Jack Frost! He pinched his nose with a bony finger and plunged his face into the water.

"I am definitely *not* pleased!" he gurgled. "You ruin everything!"

The smallest fish from the school nudged Rachel with his fin.

"I think Jack Frost needs more knee tickles," he suggested. "Don't you?"

Jack Frost spluttered with rage, then tried to stomp back to the boathouse.

Dozens of silvery fish followed behind him, nibbling at his knees.

"Don't go that way . . ." called Kirsty, her eyes twinkling.

". . . it's full of weeds!" finished Rachel.

Jack Frost was in no mood to listen to anyone. The tickly fish were really bugging him and his mermaid outfit was getting harder and harder to walk in. He took another step forward, straight into the clump of slimy weeds. Jack Frost fell backward into the water, landing with a mighty splash.

Kirsty, Rachel, and Lacey started giggling.

"He won't bother us anymore tonight," said Kirsty. "We should get ready for the ball back at Tiptop Castle."

Lacey nodded enthusiastically and opened her eyes wide. "May I ask you one last thing?"

Kirsty and Rachel both nodded.

"Will you come with me to Fairyland first?" asked Lacey. "There's a surprise waiting for you!"

A Fairy Tale Ending

Kirsty and Rachel's journey to Fairyland took place in the blink of an eye. The very second they left, time stopped in the human world. In that magical moment Lacey whisked the girls back to Fairy Tale Lane, the little winding street where she and the rest of the Fairy Tale Fairies lived. Julia, Eleanor, Faith, Rita, Gwen,

and Aisha were all waiting to greet
them. Two very important royal guests
were there as well. Kirsty and Rachel
flushed with pride—King Oberon and
Queen Titania were standing in the
road, flanked by a row of frog footmen!

"Good afternoon, Your Majesties," the
girls said politely, bobbing down into
curtseys.

The queen smiled at them. "We owe
you our heartfelt thanks," she said

warmly. "You've put the magic back into our fairy tales. Now children everywhere can enjoy these wonderful stories once more."

King Oberon nodded regally, then beckoned for Kirsty and Rachel to walk with him. "We'd like to repay your kindness," he continued, "with a small kindness of our own."

The king came to a stop outside Faith the Cinderella Fairy's house. Cinderella's Fairy Godmother opened the front door.

"These are for you," she announced, holding out two beautiful ball gowns. "I know you'll look spellbinding in them!"

"They're amazing," gushed Rachel, holding her dress up for size. It was a silk gown stitched in the softest powder blue with a matching satin sash.

Kirsty's dress was made out of smooth green velvet. It had a floaty net skirt that rustled beautifully whenever it moved.

"I feel like a fairy tale princess!" she declared. "Thank you all so much."

The Fairy Tale Fairies gathered around the girls, taking turns to give them hugs.

"Now, you've got a ball to go to," announced Lacey, blowing a fairy kiss to them both. "Have a magical evening. Good-bye, Kirsty. Good-bye, Rachel!"

With a flurry of sparkles and fairy dust, the visit was over. A little while later, the girls stepped into the Tiptop Castle ballroom. The Fairy Tale Ball was about to begin!

Kirsty looked down. She was already wearing the new ball gown from Cinderella's Fairy Godmother! Her hair was curled into ringlets and it glittered with a sparkly tiara.

Rachel looked lovely, too, the blue gems on her dress matching her eyes perfectly.

"Are you ready?" she asked. "Let's dance!"

The girls made their way over to the dance floor, holding their skirts up with their hands. Over at the dining table, Mr. and Mrs. Walker and Mr. and Mrs. Tate were chatting and nibbling party food. As soon as they spotted the girls, they gave them a big wave.

The music began to play, and Kirsty and Rachel felt like princesses again. They whirled and twirled around and around on the dance floor all night long.

"I don't want the week to end." Kirsty sighed.

Rachel nodded. "It really has been an enchanting vacation, hasn't it?"

Rosie, one of the festival organizers, thanked everyone for coming and pointed up to the ceiling. Suddenly, hundreds of golden balloons floated onto the dance floor! The guests whooped and cheered, batting balloons into the air around them.

"It's been a magical party," said Rosie, "and I can only think of one way to end it . . . with a bedtime story!"

"We've got the perfect book," said Kirsty, putting up her hand.

"Oh yes," added Rachel. "May we go and get it?"

Rosie thought it was a wonderful idea. She spread out blankets on the ballroom floor and the children sat down to hear the story. Kirsty and Rachel dashed up to their tower bedroom to get *The Fairies' Book of Fairy Tales*.

"Here it is," said Kirsty, lifting the sparkly book off the shelf.

"We've got a minute or two," whispered Rachel. "Let's take a look inside."

Kirsty opened the front cover and then flicked through the pages. All their favorite fairy tales were there, told in magical words and pictures. Near the

end of the book, the friends came across
a wonderful ocean scene. It showed a
fine ship sailing on a
moonlit night.

"There's the
Little Mermaid!"
Rachel beamed,
pointing to the
water.

Kirsty was
thrilled to see her
back where she belonged.

"What a wonderful week with the
fairies," she said. "It's been an adventure
from start to finish!"

"Yes," agreed Rachel, "an adventure
with a fabulous, fairy tale ending!"

RAINBOW magic™

SPECIAL EDITION

Rachel and Kirsty have found all of the
Fairy Tale Fairies' missing magic objects.
Now it's time for them to help

Blossom
the Flower Girl Fairy!

Join their next adventure in this
special sneak peek . . .

A Fairy Godmother

"Isn't it the most beautiful dress you've ever seen?" Rachel Walker said with a sigh as she tucked a blond curl behind her ear.

Her best friend, Kirsty Tate, nodded dreamily. "Oh, it is!" she exclaimed.

The dress was a magnificent white wedding gown covered in sparkling rhinestones and delicate lace. Rachel's aunt Angela held it in front of her as she twirled around playfully.

"You look just like a princess!" Rachel told her aunt.

Aunt Angela laughed. "I'm no princess," she told her niece. "I'm more of a fairy godmother. I make dreams come true!"

That was the truth. Aunt Angela was a wedding planner. It was her job to organize weddings down to the tiniest detail, and she was very good at it. Her company, Fairy Tale Weddings, was incredibly successful.

Rachel and Kirsty exchanged a smile at the mention of fairy godmothers. The two friends knew a lot about fairies. They had first met fairies while vacationing on Rainspell Island. Now they had many fairy friends and had visited Fairyland lots of times. Jack Frost and his mischievous goblins caused a lot of problems there, and Rachel and Kirsty were the fairies' secret helpers.

In fact, that's what the girls were doing today—being helpful! Aunt Angela had hired them to be her wedding planning assistants. Today they were at the hotel where the wedding party was staying, in case Aunt Angela needed two extra pairs of hands.

The next day's wedding was to be Tippington's largest of the year. The wedding was so big there were going to be six flower girls. Rachel and Kirsty weren't as experienced as Aunt Angela, but the girls had been bridesmaids in Kirsty's cousin Esther's wedding, so they knew a thing or two about brides and bouquets.

"This wedding is going to be amazing, Aunt Angela," Rachel said happily. "I just know it!"

RAINBOW magic™

Which Magical Fairies Have You Met?

- ❏ The Rainbow Fairies
- ❏ The Weather Fairies
- ❏ The Jewel Fairies
- ❏ The Pet Fairies
- ❏ The Dance Fairies
- ❏ The Music Fairies
- ❏ The Sports Fairies
- ❏ The Party Fairies
- ❏ The Ocean Fairies
- ❏ The Night Fairies
- ❏ The Magical Animal Fairies
- ❏ The Princess Fairies
- ❏ The Superstar Fairies
- ❏ The Fashion Fairies
- ❏ The Sugar & Spice Fairies
- ❏ The Earth Fairies
- ❏ The Magical Crafts Fairies
- ❏ The Baby Animal Rescue Fairies
- ❏ The Fairy Tale Fairies

■SCHOLASTIC

Find all of your favorite fairy friends at
scholastic.com/rainbowmagic

HiT entertainment

SCHOLASTIC and associated logos are trademarks and/or registered trademarks of Scholastic Inc. © 2015 Rainbow Magic Limited. HIT and the HIT Entertainment logo are trademarks of HIT Entertainment Limited.

RMFAIRY13

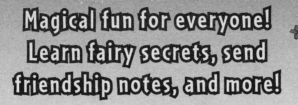

Magical fun for everyone!
Learn fairy secrets, send
friendship notes, and more!

SCHOLASTIC and associated
logos are trademarks and/or
registered trademarks of Scholastic Inc.
© 2015 Rainbow Magic Limited.
HIT and the HIT Entertainment logo
are trademarks of HIT Entertainment
Limited.

HIT entertainment

www.scholastic.com/rainbowmagic

RMACTIV4

RAINBOW magic™

Which Magical Fairies Have You Met?

- ☐ Joy the Summer Vacation Fairy
- ☐ Holly the Christmas Fairy
- ☐ Kylie the Carnival Fairy
- ☐ Stella the Star Fairy
- ☐ Shannon the Ocean Fairy
- ☐ Trixie the Halloween Fairy
- ☐ Gabriella the Snow Kingdom Fairy
- ☐ Juliet the Valentine Fairy
- ☐ Mia the Bridesmaid Fairy
- ☐ Flora the Dress-Up Fairy
- ☐ Paige the Christmas Play Fairy
- ☐ Emma the Easter Fairy
- ☐ Cara the Camp Fairy
- ☐ Destiny the Rock Star Fairy
- ☐ Belle the Birthday Fairy

- ☐ Olympia the Games Fairy
- ☐ Selena the Sleepover Fairy
- ☐ Cheryl the Christmas Tree Fairy
- ☐ Florence the Friendship Fairy
- ☐ Lindsay the Luck Fairy
- ☐ Brianna the Tooth Fairy
- ☐ Autumn the Falling Leaves Fairy
- ☐ Keira the Movie Star Fairy
- ☐ Addison the April Fool's Day Fairy
- ☐ Bailey the Babysitter Fairy
- ☐ Natalie the Christmas Stocking Fairy
- ☐ Lila and Myla the Twins Fairies
- ☐ Chelsea the Congratulations Fairy
- ☐ Carly the School Fairy
- ☐ Angelica the Angel Fairy
- ☐ Blossom the Flower Girl Fairy

3 stories in each one!

SCHOLASTIC and associated logos are trademarks and/or registered trademarks of Scholastic Inc. © 2015 Rainbow Magic Limited. HIT and the HIT Entertainment logo are trademarks of HIT Entertainment Limited.

■SCHOLASTIC

Find all of your favorite fairy friends at
scholastic.com/rainbowmagic

HiT entertainment

RMSPECIAL17